Francesco

THERE IS ALWAYS A REASON,

MARESCIALLO MAGGIO

translated by Jane Gruchy

Characters

MARESCIALLO FRANCO MAGGIO, 42, single, graying, Chief of the Viserba Carabinieri.

MARESCIALLO FERRO, Maggio's deputy, a big man with a big appetite.

LIA, a carabiniere stationed in Viserba; very smart.

DEGLIACE, another carabiniere stationed in Viserba; matter-of-fact and efficient.

ELVIO MARECCHIA, an honest farmer, recently divorced from a faithless wife.

MARY JANE HUTCHINSON, 24, blonde and beautiful.

KATE HUTCHINSON, her sister.

CIRO CARCIANTE, 35, Neapolitan fixer and small-time drug dealer, works the Rimini clubs.

PASQUALE CAMMARATA, fraudster and pusher.

ASCLEPIO POSITANO, the Prosecutor.

CAPTAIN SALTAFOSSO, Commander of the Rimini Carabinieri headquartered at Destra del Porto.

MARESCIALLI RANUCCI and PASCHETTA, a symbiotic detective team from Destra del Porto.

GENERAL CANTAMESSA, Commander of the Emilia Romagna Legion of the Carabinieri.

MARESCIALLO PIERVITTI, a colleague of Maggio's in Bologna.

MARESCIALLO ZITIELLO, a colleague of Maggio's in Naples.

NATALE, an old gangster resident in Rimini.

THE GYPSY GANG:

BRUNO, the boss.

TESLA, his woman.

TANO, the oldest.

YURI, the son.

JAKI, the youngest.

SELMA PARI, chief editor of Romagna Oggi, a local newspaper.

VISERBA, formerly a village to the north of Rimini, now absorbed into the urban area, bordered to the west by lush countryside, to the south by the Marecchia River, to the north by Via Tolemaide. Intensive holiday-making east of the railroad, farming west of the SS16 highway, small-scale industry between the railroad and the highway. Reworked geographically and emotionally, the streets and the atmosphere are part real and part imaginary, the period part contemporary and part retro.

DESTRA DEL PORTO, headquarters of the Rimini Carabinieri.

PARADISO, the imaginary club where a crucial part of the story is set, located between Via Tolemaide and Via Emilia.

VIA TOLEMAIDE, links the road along the seafront to the Rimini Nord toll booth on the A14 freeway.

VIA EMILIA, runs from Rimini to Bologna: the southern part.

VIA ORSOLETO, the Broadway of the Viserba countryside; very long, it winds through the farming district.

***

Some of the characters presented here are the protagonists of the crime mystery novel "Double Murder For Maresciallo Maggio" and don't appear in the following stories.

INTRODUCTION

The collection contains the first three episodes of Maresciallo Maggio, in chronological order.

These short stories were written over a two-year period, obeying the strict canons stipulated for writing competitions. They show the evolution of both the character and the narrative structure, which is one reason why I wanted to republish them without any substantial changes.

The first episode, *The Telltale Phone*, marks the character's debut and, from my point of view, he immediately appears the way I had imagined him. I wanted a real person, not a cliché, much less a propaganda figure: someone capable of approaching issues large and small with the same method, as critical of himself as he is of others.

Atypical characters are common now in Italian fiction, so atypical their anomalies have become the norm, homogenizing instead of differentiating them, sometimes to the point of banality. The panorama offers an abundance of Police Chiefs, deputy Police Chiefs and deputy commissioners, right down to the ordinary policeman, whereas the figure of the Maresciallo in the popular imagination is relegated to a bravura turn for the actor or a mere caricature.

My old friend Maggio came to life outside the clichés and the elegies. He is critical, but doesn't despise any aspect of what he does, familiar with the evils of the world and more of a spectator than a protagonist; in a word, he is aware.

I wanted this to show through, confiding in the understanding of the public and trusting that any qualities I may have as a narrator will be honed by experience.

Francesco Zampa

THE TELLTALE PHONE

Maresciallo Maggio was seated at his desk, staring silently at the phone, which was also silent. It was almost eight o'clock in the evening. He waited a few minutes, then got up, still looking at the phone, and headed towards the exit, switched off the lights, opened the door and stepped outside, closing it behind him. The moment he inserted the key and turned it, the phone started ringing. He checked his watch - three minutes past eight, hesitated for a second, then reopened the door and went back inside. *It might be important*, he thought, as he went to respond. He took the call directly from the guard's desk.

«Carabinieri Viserba,» he said, in a calm, firm voice.

«Good evening, sir, I was looking for the Maresciallo... is he in?»

The tone was subdued, almost a whisper, and hesitant, tentative. The *Maresciallo*, thought Maggio. Even though he knew by now that people in small towns always ask for the maresciallo, he couldn't help noting it every time.

«Speaking, sir. What can I do for you?»

«Maresciallo! It's you! This is Icio from the Gabbiano* Beach Club. Do you remember me? Last year, my cousin's girlfriend... «and he launched into a series of details and circumstances and relationships to identify himself. This was also normal.

---

*The "Seagull".

«Listen, Maresciallo,» the man continued, his voice still low, but the tone now more serious, «Maresciallo, there's a guy poking around inside a car in front of the beach club, in the car park... I mean, there's broken glass on the asphalt, Maresciallo... there's not a lot of light, but I'm quite close. He hasn't noticed me.»

«Stay where you are and don't let him see you. I'll be right over.» Now he knew who it was. The Gabbiano, Icio, thin, fortyish, tanned obviously, very moderately hard-working, a lifeguard forever, a born and bred Romagnolo*, always chasing women. Maggio hung up, found the keys of the official car, and rushed out.

He realized he wasn't carrying his gun, but he knew (and in part hoped) that it was rarely needed. Anyway, there was no time now. The Gabbiano was fairly close, about 10 minutes away. There wasn't much traffic at that hour, but it wasn't advisable to go too fast along the seafront road. The season hadn't started yet, but there were people around. He recognized in the distance the big familiar silhouette of Ferro, his invaluable deputy, strolling along with headphones over his ears. Maggio slowed down, stopped beside him and lowered the passenger window.

«Get in,» he said, «I'll explain on the way.» Ferro was already getting in. Even with his headphones on, he'd realised that something urgent was up as soon as the car pulled over. It wasn't unusual. Once he was seated, he put the radio headset into the glove box. They set off again immediately. On the way, Maggio summarised the phone call he'd just received and soon after they arrived at the Gabbiano. They observed the scene for a few seconds before getting out.

---

*Inhabitant of Emilia-Romagna.

The street turned off the Lungomare, the main road running along the seafront, and passed between two apartment buildings before ending in a small parking lot in front of the entrance to the beach club. A Lancia Ypsilon was parked there, next to the door that led into the bar and through it to the beach, but there was no one around. The car was facing away from the sea. It had been imperfectly reverse-parked, sideways across two parking spaces. Shards of glass from the driver's window lay in the shadow cast by the car on the asphalt: it had not been moved. Traces of blood were visible on the door frame on the same side.

A small awning window, slightly ajar, gave directly onto the Ypsilon. The beach club was closed, but the piled-up furniture, the boards unnailed from the windows now leaning against the walls, a few half-open tins of paint, and the brooms, mops and brushes all announced that the preparatory activity for the coming season had begun, and very recently. «Maresciallo! Maresciallo!» Icio's voice interrupted Maggio's thoughts. He was coming out the back door of the club. Maggio noticed that he was clean and dressed to the nines, but his face was pale.

«Ciao, Icio. Everything okay?» said Maggio. Ferro greeted him with a nod.

«I didn't know what to do ... he went that way...» He pointed to the lane that led between the buildings to the Lungomare. He went on, «...I was, uhm, ...tidying up something over there... in the changing rooms..., he pointed with his thumb behind him, without turning around. He was staring wide-eyed in the direction of the footpath.

«What did he look like?» asked Maggio.

«Well... tall... thin... I don't know... maybe he took something... I mean, maybe he had something in his hand... I don't know...»

Maggio had a quick look inside the car, being careful not to step on the glass. Someone had injured themselves on that frame. The radio was still there. Apart from the glass, nothing seemed to be out of place. He set off along the footpath towards the Lungomare, even though he realized that about fifty metres further on, where it entered the main road, it would be practically impossible to find any trace of the fugitive in the hustle and bustle that preceded the dinner hour. But you never know, so he gave it a go.

«Ferro, you take care of the car, track down the owner, it's probably a woman. I'll see you at the station, I'm going to walk back.»

«Why a woman?»

«I saw at least two bags and three pairs of sandals inside, and look how it's parked.» He didn't say this ironically, it was what he had seen. He remembered the cartoons about the content of women's thoughts. He walked along the footpath. As expected, it was sufficiently crowded to make it hard to simply choose which side to walk along. At the corner of the footpath and the street, there were kids playing football under the watchful eye of a grandfather sitting to one side of the building's small courtyard.

«*Ohé, burdèl*! *BURDÈL*!*» he called out to them in an improbable version of the local dialect.

---

*"Hey, you kids!"

«It's the Maresciallo! The Maresciallo! The carabinieri! The carabinieri!» a ragged chorus of voices yelled back in reply, then they gathered around him.

«He did it! It was him! No, it was him! Arrest him!» They went on like that for a while, then quietened down as curiosity got the better of them.

«*Ohé, burdèl*, did you see somebody running out of here a few minutes ago, out of the lane leading to the sea?» He waved his arms to keep their attention. The answer was another ragged chorus: «I saw him! No, I did! He went in there, he was a Moroccan!»

«No, he went that way, he was white.»

They pointed in opposite directions. «He was white! He was holding his arm!»

«No, he was Moroccan and he only had one arm!»

Maggio realized there wasn't much more to be learnt from them, so he said goodbye and headed back to the station along Via Sacramora, the road parallel to the Lungomare.

A few minutes later, as he was walking past the *piadineria*[*] in Viserba Monte, he saw a Mercedes, a 1990 model or thereabouts, rather battered and, more to the point, crammed full of all sorts of things: beach mats, towels, tissues, but also saucepans and T-shirts. Two Moroccans were sitting at a nearby table; one was devouring a piadina with prosciutto; another, with sausages, was on its way. Both men had half-empty mugs of dark beer in front of them; a third mug, full, was standing by. In the centre of the table, two packets of MS

---

[*]A small shop selling *piadine*, the traditional fast food of Romagna, a flat bread served with a wide variety of fillings.

patiently waited their turn. At the end of a hard day's work, Allah the Merciful understands and forgives those who fall into temptation in the corrupt world of the infidels. Maggio went over. Eros, the owner, came forward to greet him, while Babi and Lu, the two waitresses, one dark, the other red-haired, smiled at him mischievously.

«*Buonasera*, Maresciallo, can I offer you something? Pear, peach?»

The most alcoholic thing Maggio ever ordered from Eros were fruit juices. *A pineapple juice* or *succo de ananas*, popped out occasionally, and that *de* instead of *di* was the reason why Eros always mimicked what he thought was a Roman inflection. But Maggio, despite that slight lexical imprecision, was neither Roman nor from Lazio.

«Ciao, Eros. No thanks. How long have those two been here?» He indicated them with a glance.

«About an hour,» Eros replied, without turning around. «They've come from Rimini.» Rimini was in the opposite direction to the site of the theft. Maggio went over to their table.

«Worked hard today, eh?» They nodded, and kept eating.

«Where's your friend, the one missing an arm?» He gave it a try, without thinking too much about it.

«He worked with us today,» one of the them replied. «Now he's gone *chéz la Police*.»

Maggio didn't have time to be amazed that his hunch had been correct because the second statement made him much more curious.

«You mean to the station, to me? And why was that?» he continued.

«To report a crime.»

Maggio stopped for a moment to think. It wasn't unusual for these Moroccans to take bizarre stands. They spent the day selling carpets, the evening eating, drinking and smoking, and the next day it started all over again.

He said goodbye, drank a glass of water under the satisfied gaze of Eros and walked briskly back to the station. When he was almost there, he got a call from Ferro.

«There's a certain Miftah here who says he knows who broke the window of that car.»

«I'm on my way,» said Maggio.

The placid lapping of the waves accompanied the restorative quiet of the dinner hour, inviting body and spirit to a peaceful communion of the senses and to love, rather than the investigation that was beginning to loom ahead. He climbed the stairs to the station, unlocked the door and went into the office. The Moroccan was sitting down; he had only one arm, and he was sweaty, dirty, and wearing wooden clogs. He looked like someone who had just finished work. Ferro stood next to him, leaning on the window sill. Maggio went over and offered the man a cigarette, which he accepted. Maggio pulled another one out for himself, then lit them both with his lighter. They inhaled the first puff deeply. Behind them, red on white, a NO SMOKING sign admonished them impotently. Ferro went into the other room, he couldn't stand cigarette smoke, reappearing briefly just to say his piece:

«Let's put him under arrest then go to Mazza's.» Mazza's was the restaurant on the state highway favoured by truckers because of its ample parking area, quick service, excellent food and low prices.

«Ah,» he added, «the owner of the Ypsilon is on her way here, I tracked her down a little while ago.» The bell interrupted them; Maggio motioned to Ferro to stay where he was.

«I'll go,» he said. It was a man and a woman; she thirty-five, dark-haired and shapely, with the requisite tan; he tall, blonde, and handsome. «A good-looking couple,» thought Maggio. They both looked embarrassed; the man spoke first.

«There... they called us... about the Ypsilon...»

«It was parked near the house...», she broke in, annoyed. «They smashed the glass... and they stole my phone!» she said in a rising crescendo, finally bursting into hysterical tears. «I want it back, they must give it back! IT'S MINE!» And the tears kept flowing.

«Calm down, dear; you'll see... we'll find it, we'll find it... sit down... come on... «His voice was more self-possessed, and he seemed even more embarrassed. But every effort to console her failed, she shook him off, got even more worked up, and wouldn't listen to reason.

Maggio reflected for a moment, then turned to the Moroccan.

«Miftah,» he said, «Miftah, have you seen the lady's phone?»

Miftah maintained his upright posture and looked straight ahead.

«I don't know, boss. You going to friends' place for dinner; you see glass on ground near car; I go closer to see better... then I hear noises from the house and I run away...» He spoke an improbable but effective Franco-Italian-Moroccan.

«What noises did you hear, Miftah?»

«Soft voices, soft footsteps... if somebody comes, sees Moroccan near car with broken glass; *qui à été*? It was Moroccan! But I did not do anything, and I run away.» He could have drawn the opposite conclusion, but Maggio could hardly blame him.

«And where did you go?» asked Maggio.

«To my friends, at Viserba Monte ... I sit, I order a drink, then I think: you have only one arm, if somebody sees you they call the Police, they say that I break the glass ... so I come here first...»

«You didn't see anybody?»

«*Non*, little light, almost evening.»

Though very close to the sea, the piazzetta where the Ypsilon was parked was fairly secluded and, at that hour, very quiet. It was feasible that whispers and muffled noises could be audible.

«Did you find a cell phone?»

«No, boss, nothing, *je vous jure*; I have children, I have a wife, two wives, I work and that is all...» He continued, in Arabic, to explain his situation in detail. But his voice was fading, Maggi had already gone back to the guard's room. The couple were waiting. She was still very jittery.

«Have we finished? Can we go?» she asked, impatiently.

«Yes, we're done,» said Ferro, and handed them a copy of the complaint.

«There, let's go!» she said, addressing her husband. «Come on, get up.» So saying, she leapt to her feet, urging on her husband with a nasty slap on the forearm. Her husband's reaction was totally overwrought. Up till then he'd kept his emotions under control, but now he held back no longer.

«You be careful!» he snapped. «What do I care about your phone!» He stroked his smarting arm, as he continued to vent all the tension that suddenly seemed to have gripped him. Maggio watched the scene thoughtfully.

«Come with me,» he said. «We'll go and see if we can find the phone.» Without another word he headed towards the exit. The couple calmed down and followed him with a mixture of diffidence and curiosity. Ferro stayed behind with Miftah. They all got into the official car, and a few minutes later they were back at the Gabbiano parking area. The car was still there. The little awning window had been closed, but a light was on, evidently there was still someone inside. The moon illuminated the scene. The couple stared at each other, incredulous and suspicious, each searching for an explanation in the other's gaze.

«Which is your building?» Maggio asked the husband.

«That one there,» he said, pointing to the apartment building at the end of the lane, to the right of the small courtyard where the kids had been playing ball. *Opposite the piadineria, just as the kids said*, thought Maggio. He took out his phone, slipped the copy of the complaint out of the lady's hands then dialed a number. She stared at him attentively, her eyes narrowed, while her husband looked increasingly tense. Neither of them fully understood what was happening. An unmistakable, irreverent, cacophonous ringtone broke the silence, but it didn't check the growing tension.

She was the first to speak. «It's MY PHONE! IT'S MY PHONE! Where is it? WHERE IS IT?»

The sound was coming from the premises of the Gabbiano.

«Icio, you can come out,» said Maggio. An uncertain shadow persisted for a few seconds in the beam of light from above the doorway; it was Icio who swiftly emerged with the phone in his hand.

«Good… good evening…»

It was a laudable attempt, but it was definitely not a good evening.
Her flushed face began to pale, suddenly she dropped her gaze.

The husband's eyes widened, then narrowed into a scowl as, livid with rage, he exclaimed:

«YOU! Damn you! I knew it! Now I understand!» He threw himself headlong at Icio, arms and hands outstretched. Maggio grabbed him with surgical precision by the right forearm, tightening his grip on exactly the same spot where his wife had struck him shortly before. There followed an unrestrained howl of pain. The husband stopped abruptly, covering his arm with his left hand by way of protection.

«Give me the phone, Icio,» said Maggio. «Come with me, we're going back to the station.»

The following evening, Maggio was doing his usual run; his schedule involved 50 not-too-demanding minutes along the Lungomare in the direction of the children's holiday camps, where there was almost no traffic and few people around. On the way he bumped into Gionis, the lifeguard from the 42 Beach Club, another authentic product of Romagna.

«Ciao, Gionis.»

«Ciao, Maresciallo. I heard about the phone business... come on, everyone knew about the lady... well, yes, I mean, about her and Icio ... she didn't get along with her husband, and Icio's not one to say no to...»

«And you are?» The other smiled smugly. He took it as a compliment.

«But how did you know it was him?»

«He suspected that his wife was cheating on him but she always acted with the utmost prudence. In a fit of jealousy, he went out looking for her. He saw the parked car and he couldn't work out where she was. He went and looked inside it, saw the phone in the glove box and decided to get his hands on it to verify his suspicions. It's very unusual for a woman to go anywhere without a phone; if she's cheating, even more so. It seemed like a golden opportunity to him. Blind with rage, he smashed the window, leaned in to grab it and, in the heat of the moment, cut his arm. Maybe he started going through her address book, the most recent calls, the messages, all still there; but, suddenly, he heard a noise. It was Miftah on his way to meet up with his friends. He's not a thief; he immediately panicked, got confused, threw the phone into the car where it ended up under the pedals or on the mat, and ran off along the lane towards home. A few seconds later, Miftah arrived and saw the car with the broken glass. Intrigued, he went over to have a look. In the silence of the evening, he heard noises and whispers. He couldn't know this, but it was Icio and the lady indulging in a little dalliance, or talking, or maybe Icio had simply suggested she hide because he'd just seen her husband wandering around outside. Miftah realised that he'd better leave, because it would have been very difficult for him to explain his presence if anyone saw him there. So he walked away, faster now, and he too slipped into the lane, but when he came out, he turned in the opposite direction. Finally, she came out, too. She saw the smashed car window but she was afraid that someone would see her with Icio. She couldn't call her husband, or not right away, otherwise she'd have had to explain what she was doing in the changing rooms at the Gabbiano. She decided to go home as if nothing had happened. But then she realized that she was missing her phone. At precisely that point, Ferro tracked them down and informed them that there was no phone in the car. She feared that whoever had taken it would nosey around; the husband couldn't understand how it had disappeared, maybe he thought of Miftah. But both of them lied and were frightened of being found out if they asked any questions. Meanwhile, Icio, once he was alone, had gone outside to see what had happened, had taken a quick look in the car and immediately found the phone that had been tossed back inside. He took it, thinking he'd find a way to return it or to prevent somebody really stealing it. Who knows, maybe she was still there when we arrived.»

«Heavens above! But how can you be sure? Go on, they told you about it!»

«It's just my theory. Miftah talked about broken glass, not about phones or thefts. But the husband had hurt his arm; he knew the phone was still in the car and he knew it would be found. She was worried only about being found out.» The other man stared at him. «But Icio did confirm it all!»

Just then, Ferro arrived on his Vespa.

«How much longer are you going to run for?» he asked.

«I'm heading back now. Why?» replied Maggio.

«Alright, I'll wait for you in front of the station. Ciao, Gionis.»

Maggio returned a few minutes later, took a shower and changed. He went outside; Ferro was already there with the Vespa.

«Look at this,» he said, handing him a copy of the *Carlino Rimini*.
Maggio could already guess what it was. The article was on the inner pages, in the local news section. The title was not particularly original:

BETRAYED BY A TELLTALE PHONE

The subheading gave a little more detail: *Jealous husband discovers wife's infidelity thanks to her cell phone.* He already knew the rest. Ferro handed him a helmet. As he climbed onto the Vespa another scooter drew up beside them. It was Babi and Lu. They had just closed the *piadineria*.

«Ciao, *ragazzi*. And what are you two up to now?» In Rimini, everyone was a *ragazzo*, a kid, until they were fifty. And even afterwards. Maggio and Ferro looked at each other. Ferro spoke first.

«We're going for a bite to eat at Mazza's. Want to come with us?»

«Sure we do!» replied the *ragazze*. «Let's go to Mazza's!»

A NASTY BUSINESS

Giordano got out of the driver's side and stood stock-still in front of him, blocking his escape route. The black man was impressively built, but although Giordano was less athletic, his bulk commanded respect and caution. Maggio came round the other side of the car and was beside them. The black man had a moment of hesitation, then threw his bag to the ground: out of the open zipper spilled fake Lacoste polos, crumpled banknotes and some loose change. He then hurled himself at the obstacle that looked easier to overcome - Maggio, in other words, who made ready to absorb the inevitable impact. He found himself on the ground, on his back, with the black man trying to pull himself up from his hands and knees and regain speed by passing over him. Maggio, forgetting every self-defense technique he'd ever learned, more or less, years before, grabbed one of his legs and hung on with difficulty while he yelled to Giordano: «THE HANDCUFFS! THE HANDCUFFS.» It wasn't clear how he was going to be able to use them. The black man was trying to jerk himself free from his awkward position, leveraging the ground with one leg, the other on Maggio's arms. Maggio looked round for Giordano, turned towards him, then instantly shut his eyes tight. Giordano's entire bulk flew over him, obscuring his view and landing peremptorily on the black man with such force he was knocked to the ground. It was more of a tackle than a capture. Maggio drew himself up into a sitting position, for starters, then ran over to the other two with the handcuffs open. The black man didn't want to know about that and was still struggling on the ground, but there was no way he could free himself with Giordano's knee planted firmly in the middle of his back, a knee that was spokesman for almost a hundred kilos. His muscles still quivering from the enormous and unexpected effort, Maggio managed to handcuff the man to the nearest lamppost.

It had all lasted a matter of seconds. A curious crowd had gathered around the patrol and the man tied to the lamp post, now anything but indomitable. Maggio stood up and straightened his uniform; fortunately his cap had remained in the car. Giordano, however, was already in order. He seemed to have made no great effort.

«Shall we load him aboard?» he asked.

«Wait,» replied Maggio. «I want to understand what happened first.»

Headquarters had called a few minutes before midnight on a beautiful June evening. *A fight, they said, go and have a look.* Via Porto Palos, the Lungomare, the pizzeria; they were about to go back to the station, it was the end of their shift, but now that the season had begun, it was by no means unusual for them to be called out at the last moment, and even after.

Some of the spectators, recovering from their surprise, were beginning to wonder why the man was tied up; others were ranting at him, and others still were growling at the two carabinieri. Off a little to one side, Pasquale, the Neapolitan waiter, was raising his eyebrows more than was natural while simultaneously widening his eyes, fixed on Maggio, and perceptibly bobbing his head towards a person seated nearby. He might as well have just pointed at him. Maggio, now straightened up, passed unperturbed through the small crowd. The guy sitting at a table outside the pizzeria, smoking in front of a beer mug, was Lonis Campedelli, a thirty-five-old born-and-bred local, farmer and hunter.

«Buonasera, Maresciallo,» Lonis began by saying, with an insincere smile. «Can I offer you anything?» he continued.

«Maybe some other time,» replied Maggio. «What happened?» Three people were moving closer to the table, apparently unafraid of disturbing. Maggio sat down at the table with Lonis, blocking their view and turning his back on them. The three stopped a couple of metres away, unsure as to how to procede.

«I was just sitting here, having a beer,» his eyes narrowed as he looked in the direction of the handcuffed guy, the black pupils small but alert. «That guy came over to try and sell me a fake T-shirt. I *told* him I didn't want it, he moved on; then all of a sudden he turned round and came back threatening me in some incomprehensible language. He wanted to punch me out, so I got up to defend myself.»

As he listened, Maggio saw Giordano pick up the black man's bag, push the half-fallen-out T-shirts back in, close the zipper and place it in the boot of the patrol car.

«My friends put themselves between me and him and he attacked them. Then you two arrived and he tried to run away, but you caught him, the bastard.»

Maggio didn't like that last word; he wanted to hear facts, not comments. That assertion betrayed a desire for complicity, an unfounded sense of verifying an assent that was in no way to be taken for granted. Maggio made no comment. But what struck him even more forcibly was the creeping racism typical of Lonis and his cronies, a warped sentiment that grew like a weed among the fruits of an affluence that had its origin in the proverbial Romagnola tradition of enthusiasm for hard work. A sentiment which meant that anyone who arrived there attracted by that affluence was greeted with diffidence, if he was an honest worker, or open hostility, even when they were desperate people come halfway around the world, and not necessarily thieves or dishonest.

«We're going to the station,» Maggio cut him short. «You're coming with us.»

He went back to the handcuffed guy without waiting for a reply. He could observe him better now: he was tall and athletic, black as ebony. Head down, he was lost in thought. Maggio went up to him.

«What's your name?» he asked.

«Moussa,» he replied.

«Moussa, we're going to the police station now to see what's to be done. Are you okay?»

«*Oui*... yes...», he nodded.

Under Giordano's watchful eye, Maggio removed the handcuffs, took his arm and headed towards the car. Astonishing everybody, Moussa whirled around and tried to head butt the light pole to which he'd been handcuffed only shortly before, without much conviction if truth were told. Giordano's mighty arms firmly encircled him and this time he got into the car. The thronging crowd parted to let them through, somebody shouted *GO BACK WHERE YOU CAME FROM, NIGGER*, while others had it in for the carabinieri, and others still were getting too close to the car. They were all peaceable people, but there are situations that can flare up in an instant and, when everything seems under control, spread like wildfire for a few long seconds, sometimes leading to irreparable damage. Maggio knew that well.

«We should go.»

He thought a lot of the aggression was just posturing, but whether it was matter of conviction or only simple emulation, the end result was likely to be the same. Just then a second patrol car pulled up.

«Need any help?» asked the patrol chief. It was Lonetti, a creep with a flamboyant lifestyle who was often violent. He did his job, but Maggio didn't like him.

«Bring that one in.» He pointed to Lonis, standing near the chair. Lonetti opened the back door of the car, made room on the seat then turned to Lonis, motioning with his head for him to get in. The arrogant gesture and the authoritarian, almost disgusted stare extinguished any hypothetical reaction aimed at avoiding ending the evening at the station in the company of four carabinieri and a detainee. Lonis got his cigarettes, left his half-finished beer and climbed in.

When they arrived at the station, Maggio went into the office with Moussa while Lonis stayed in the waiting room with Giordano and Lonetti. He sat Moussa down; he seemed calmer now, Maggio took off the handcuffs. He searched for his cigarettes, he left an open packet in every place he smoked in, found them, lit one and inhaled slowly. He opened the window that looked out over the sea, waited a couple of minutes, stubbed out the butt in the blackened ashtray then turned back to Moussa.

«So, do you want to tell me what happened?»

«I went there to sell, boss. Every morning I have thirty T-shirts in my bag, I pay 9 euros for them, I sell them for ten or eleven. At the end of the week I send the money to my family in Senegal. I have six children.» He paused.

«Go on,» Maggio encouraged him.

«I arrived at the pizzeria and I went round the tables to try and sell the last ones, boss. I asked him. He said *I don't want anything*, I moved on. From behind I heard *Go home, you dirty nigger*.» I would've bet on that, thought Maggio.

«They thought I couldn't understand, but I have a university degree, I've had an education, you know, boss. I went back; I asked him to *répète-le, répète-le*. He said *what do you want? what do you want?* He kept quiet, but I was sure it was him, I recognized the voice. I asked him again even louder. Then two or three others got between us, he stayed sitting down. They came closer, they looked at me. I kept yelling, they yelled too. I was scared, but so were they. They didn't come any closer. *Piss off, piss off*, they said, *go back to Africa, nigger*. I felt them grab me by the arms. Another one arrived, he said to them *calm down, calm down*, and to me *why don't you just go back to where you came from and make trouble there?* It went on like that for a while, they were muttering and looking at me, so I shoved them, I could feel them hitting me on the back, spitting at me. My bag fell to the ground open, someone started kicking it. I tried to struggle free, but then you arrived.»

His voice was still agitated, he was breathing fast, he couldn't calm down. Maggio sensed that it wasn't just because he had been arrested. He walked around him, the shirt he was wearing was clammy with sweat. Impossible to establish if there was spit on it as well.

«It would've been better for you just to leave,» commented Maggio. «Now we have to arrest you, because you resisted an officer.»

«But I haven't done anything. I didn't want to come here like this, I am ashamed, you know? What do I say to my wife, boss? That the *police* arrested me?» he replied proudly, then lowered his head.

It was the first time Maggio had heard anything like this: a person who's been arrested who isn't worried about the charges, but is ashamed. More or less aware of it, he was racist, too: he took it for granted that a poverty-stricken immigrant would have no scruples about what he did to survive. He re-evaluated Moussa's description of his business: 30 T-shirts a day; if all went well, that meant thirty-forty euros. Not a lot, he thought, but not chicken feed, either. However he had to live on it, pay the rent on his room, eat and send something home. Not easy, he thought.

Maggio left Moussa in his office and went into the other room. Giordano was checking the contents of the bag while chatting with Lonis. Evidently they knew each other. Lonetti, lounging off to one side, was admiring his fingernails. Maggio didn't like excessive familiarity; not that he enjoyed playing the part of the lilywhite tough guy, but he knew that casual, superficial acquaintance was easy and deceptive, and he wanted to avoid any cause for self-reproach. His friends were few and carefully chosen, and those who knew him knew what to expect from him. Maggio motioned to Giordano to go to Moussa, he would stay in the waiting room with Lonis. It was hot, so he opened the front door to let in a bit of fresh air. Just then he saw her, or rather he saw her car pass and turn into Via dell'Amarcord. A matter of moments, even less, but enough to undermine his apparent calm. He was used to it; he knew she wasn't going to stop and he wasn't going to chase after her. He turned back to Lonis, immersing himself in the present.

«You know how it is, Maggio, they hassle you until you lose your patience. I told him that, but he...» Unsolicited, Lonis was on the attack... «Everybody knows me, they know I'm a good fellow... and in fact I'm friends with that guy, what's his name again...»

«Oh yes, a real friend,» commented Maggio.

«That's not going to get you off the hook, because I'm charging you, too. You can explain all that to the magistrate,» he continued, speaking to him aloud.

«But... no... I, what...» he stuttered.

They were interrupted by the ring of the phone. Calls during the night weren't uncommon, but everything suggested that the communication was relevant to what was happening.

«Viserba Carabinieri.» The voice of the guard catalyzed the attention of everyone present. Maggio seized the opportunity to glance outside: her Mini wasn't there; as expected, she hadn't stopped. In compensation, a few bystanders, no doubt friends of Lonis's, were patiently waiting at the gate.

The guard's voice snapped him out of it: «Maresciallo, it's Lombardi.» Lombardi had commanded the station years before; he was from the Marches, a hunter like Lonis, and had been retired for several years now. It wasn't hard to guess what he wanted.

«Ciao, Maggio. How are you?» he began.

«Ciao, Lombardi, I'm fine, yes, thank you.» The perfect time to reassure himself about my health, thought Maggio.

«You know how it is,» he continued. «That boy Lonis, we're friends ... he's a good fellow... they must have made him angry... see what you can do...» Maggio listened, none too attentively; evidently the word had spread that Lonis was at the station and that it wasn't a mere formality.

«Yes, don't worry, I know how it is,» said Maggio, and his reply licensed any interpretation. «Now, I'm sorry, I must go.» He hung up.

He reflected for a few moments about what was happening, while Lonetti finished putting Moussa's things back into the big bag. It didn't seem right to arrest him, but it wasn't up to him to decide. The law is clear, you can't resist Authority. There were a stack of people there, we don't want to look soft and so on and so forth. Yet... he had a flash of inspiration and went back to the office. He invited Moussa and Giordano to go and sit in the room next door, at a good distance from Lonis. He took down the Criminal Code, the edition with the invaluable commentaries by Pier Luigi Vigna that every maresciallo used in school, and began to turn the pages, found the article he was looking for and read the comments: intention was an essential requirement, but Moussa had run away because he was frightened of being attacked. Who wouldn't have been? There remained the fact that he'd struggled free to head butt the pole: an escape attempt? But he'd stopped immediately, saying afterwards that he was ashamed. There was room for doubt.

Maggio concluded that he would report the facts and file a complaint against both of them, but release them to await trial; the prosecutor would determine whether and what to ultimately charge them with. It resembled washing his hands of it a' la Pontius Pilate, but in actual fact, it meant assuming greater responsibility. The carabinieri intervene, thought Maggio, the Judges decide, you just have to always tell the truth. Comforted by his Solomonic decision, he went back to Moussa.

«We're not going to arrest you, don't worry, you'll be going home tonight. But it would be a good idea if you changed area for the next few days.»

Moussa listened, and appeared heartened, but didn't reply.

«Giordano, give him back his personal belongings,» said Maggio, «including the bag. Not the t-shirts, we have to confiscate those. And prepare the statement.»

Then he went into the other room; Lonetti looked as though he was losing his patience, the whole thing had gone on too long for his liking. Lonis was visibly worried.

«You can go now, you just have to appoint a lawyer.»

«A lawyer? What on earth for? He did it! They come here and do what the hell they like and hardworking people like me are the ones who pay for it, they steal our jobs, that's what they do. The heck with you, Maggio, this time you've made a big mistake!!» he whined.

«Don't worry, you can explain it all to your lawyer.»

He didn't wait for a reply because Moussa had suddenly started yelling again. Maggio raced into the other room.

«50 EUROS ARE MISSING, THERE WERE 150 EUROS IN HERE. NOW THERE ARE ONLY 100. WHERE ARE THEY?»

Moussa was flushed with rage again. Maggio looked at him, then turned to Giordano, meeting his incredulous gaze. He was holding the confiscation order and spread his arms as if to say: «I know nothing about it.» Maggio tried again to calm Moussa down. The banknote had probably fallen to the ground during the scuffle at the pizzeria. Eventually, he did quieten down, resigned to his loss. A night to forget. The two detainees left, Lonis first, to be hailed as a hero by his friends. They stood around a while outside, talking and commenting, they patted him on the back, smoking and laughing, but Lonis was not quite as jovial as the others. Finally they all went away. But Maggio waited another half hour before accompanying Moussa to the door. He looked out, the street was deserted. Not entirely convinced, he went down to the garage with Moussa, got out the official car and drove him to where he lived, not far away, off Via Sacramora. It was dark, there was no one around; Moussa got out where the small dirt track began and headed toward the old abandoned farmhouse he shared with other compatriots.

Maggio returned to the station, alone, with the uneasy feeling he hadn't got to the bottom of it. The racism they had displayed clashed with the apparently innate joviality and friendliness of the local inhabitants, and increased his conviction that it was important to maintain his detachment, a detachment he didn't enjoy, however. And what about the 50 euros, had they really disappeared? If so, where? At the pizzeria? At the station? He instinctively thought of Lonetti, his long fingernails, his gold bracelets and his frequently unorthodox ways, but he had no reason to pursue the idea any further. He parked the car in the garage and went inside, using the internal door. As he climbed the stairs, he passed by the office. Through the open door, he could see the confiscated T-shirts still lying on the desk. He went over and regarded them attentively, touched them. They were clumsy fakes, even the plastic they were wrapped in was very poor quality. He wondered whether those shirts could really throw a spanner in the works of the big brand multinationals, but the law prohibiting forgery was unambiguous: all counterfeit products were to be seized and destroyed. He stood there a few moments longer, lost in thought, then put the T-shirts back and went upstairs to bed.

Silence reigned in the sleeping quarters, the evening's business had gone on for a long time and it was late. Giordano was in his room, the light from his bedside lamp spilling through the half-closed bedroom door. Maggio's room was at the end of the corridor, to get to it he had to walk pass all the others. Not wanting to disturb anybody, he tiptoed on through the silence. But suddenly his eyes widened and he came to an abrupt halt. A jolt of adrenaline wiped away his accumulated tiredness: what he had just seen out of the corner of his eye was a pair of trousers thrown onto a chair, with a crumpled 50 Euro bill poking out of the pocket. The moment past, hoping he was wrong, he took a step backwards, stopped in the strip of light coming through the door and looked again. The massive bulk of Giordano, in his undershirt, came between him and the trousers. His face was unsmiling; they stared at each other, both waiting for the other to speak. Maggio said nothing and moved to one side to improve his line of sight: the trousers were still on the chair, the bill, if it had ever been there, was gone. He turned again towards Giordano who waited a few seconds longer, then headed to the bathroom. Maggio stayed where he was, thinking. He looked again at the chair, then at the bathroom door, undecided about what he should do. Finally, he too retired to his room.

The expression on Giordano's face kept him awake late into the night. The next day, he got up early, wrote the report on the events of the night before, including the alleged disappearance of the 50 Euro banknote, and faxed it to the Rimini Public Prosecutor with a request for the destruction of the confiscated T-shirts. That was a formality. He put on his Sam Browne belt and his cap, put the T-shirts into a plastic bag and the bag into the boot of the official car, then headed to the Carabinieri Headquarters. The guard had only just got up; he was having coffee upstairs; Maggio saw him turn away from the kitchen window but didn't place much importance on the fact.

When he got to Destra del Porto, he drove inside and parked, then walked up to the first floor. The secretary hadn't arrived yet, but

Captain Saltafosso was already at his desk, going through the reports from the night before. Maggio greeted him, asked permission to speak with him and went into the office. The captain interrupted his updating: he didn't usually see Maggio unless he summoned him himself, let alone at that early hour. Maggio explained what had happened and gave him a copy of the report. The other read it through carefully.

«I would like Giordano transferred,» said Maggio, tersely.

«What if you're mistaken?» replied Saltafosso.

«And if I'm not?»

Saltafosso looked at him. «I'll think it over.»

Maggio said goodbye and left, but instead of taking the road along the seafront, he turned inland and took Via Sacramora, the road that divided the joyous life of the coast from the countryside. A few minutes later, he arrived at the house where Moussa lived. By day he could look at it more closely. It was an isolated building, like many others, witness to an era that had come to an end, though only a few decades before. It was old, the roof was in a poor state of repair, the doors and windows barely functional. He got out of the car and walked to the main door, under the perplexed but intrigued gaze of the other Senegalese who gradually gathered around, stepping aside to let him pass. Somebody with a shoulder bag ran away, but most of them continued to stare at him; some standing, some squatting, some unsmiling. Despite it being only a little after seven, the whole community was already active, even the kids were outside playing.

He went through the main door and climbed the long flight of stairs to the first floor. The staircase was surfaced with brick tiles, old rather than antique: worn out, abandoned, then returned to service, now very much the worse for wear. The stairs led to four identical rooms that opened off a corridor with a bathroom and a kitchen at the end. The smell of stale air was very strong, but that wasn't the worst thing he found: all the rooms were crammed with individual habitations, each consisting of a mattress. Next to each one were a few clothes, a bag, a saucepan, cutlery, a few tins of rice and tuna, here and there a Koran. The electrical system, if one could call it that, was made of old, exposed ceramic knob and tube wiring, with extremely dangerous unsheathed runs and splices. It was just as well there was no electricity. The bathroom had seen better days a long time before, when just having one in the house was a luxury, but it worked. This then was where Moussa and his compatriots returned at the end of their working day; this was where they ate and rested before the next day began. And someone was taking advantage of the extreme poverty of these improvised traders. Maggio counted 34 mattresses; he knew they were paying two-three hundred euros a head, off the books, of course. But the last room was a surprise: it was the smallest, with a floor of worn, square, black and grey-flecked tiles, but there were only three beds, remade; a stone sink with dishes washed and lying face down covered with a cloth, a bedside table with paper and felt-tipped pens. Not a thing was out of place, and the hygiene was absolute. Maggio realised that he was looking at the home of a family, the hand of a loving wife and mother and an exemplary dignity. He turned to go back and saw that there were women and children lining the stairs, staring at him. Halfway up stood Moussa, also watching him with a puzzled frown. Maggio walked back down amid the silence of people retreating. He got to the car, followed closely by Moussa and a throng of curious children. He opened the boot, took out the plastic bag with the T-shirts in it and left it on the ground.

«They've been destroyed,» he said.

Then he got into the car, started the engine and went back to the station.

Late that afternoon, he put on shorts and trainers and went off to run for at least an hour before dinner. He took the road from the old rope works towards Via Orsoleto and the countryside. He was halfway there when he saw her, leaning against the car. Maggio ran past her, but their eyes met. It was enough. He slowed down, stopped, and turned back, walking. Finally, they started talking again.

ADDRESSEE UNKNOWN

The man crawled forward a little, pushing the barrel of his gun silently through the leaves, his movements slow and deliberate. Now, he could see it clearly, roughly 25 meters away. He directed the invisible line linking eye, crosshairs and rear sight to just beneath the heart of his target, who was gazing off towards the other side of the river, untroubled, from its privileged position near the bank. Delicately, the man cocked the hammer, careful not to make the slightest noise. He'd been lying in wait for two hours, he knew the terrain. Without turning around, he slid his left foot sideways a couple of centimetres, searching for the best support. As soon as it felt firm enough, he pushed back hard on the leg to create the human tripod required to provide stability for the shot. He was ready. *It's over*, he thought, *you have two more seconds*. He began to exert a constant pressure on the trigger with his index finger, as the manual dictates. But suddenly the earth gave way beneath his left heel and, deprived of that efficient buttress, his right arm jerked to one side. The barrel reared up three or four centimetres, which translated into several meters above the target's head. His finger yanked at the trigger the way exactly you're not supposed to do, and the shot exploded upwards into the clouds above.

He quickly took up his position again, but the elusive pheasant had already terminated its short flight into the nearby woods.

The hunter lay there for while, gazing towards it incredulously, then got to his knees and stood up. He looked towards the woods again. Nothing. He ran through the last few moments in his mind. The foot, the ground. He turned and looked down. A wooden board shifted slightly, a bit of earth covering it, a small hole. Inside it was a package wrapped in transparent plastic, its edges roughly sealed, almost vacuum-packed, the size of an ordinary bag of flour. It looked like flour, but it was darker and coarser.

Mrs Marecchia, thirty years old, shiny straight hair, two shapely legs that disappeared at the crucial moment into a too-short skirt and an ex-husband well past fifty who'd been under house arrest for over a year, aroused all too obvious comments. But Maggio didn't like clichés.

He had stood, leaning against the window overlooking the sea, listening to her, seated in front of his desk; he'd waited patiently for her to finish and finally he'd spoken himself. He'd now come to the conclusion of his speech.

«What we can do, *signora*? If they let him go, it means he had done his time. You were the one who laid the charges, weren't you? A year has gone by since then.»

«Yes, but straight away, just like that... .Yesterday he went out hunting again as though nothing had happened... If you could just put him back inside…,» she replied.

Inwardly Maggio winced, but only a little. How many wives would like to get rid of their husbands? Not to mention the husbands! After all, Mrs Marecchia was only being sincere. All at once, she sprang to her feet. The unassuming and embarrassed air had vanished. Two deep black eyes, suddenly malignant, bored into

Maggio's own. She moved towards him unafraid, stopping only a few inches from his face.

«You know what my friends at the hairdresser's say, Maggio? That there's a maresciallo in Viserba who's really, really hot!»

For a few seconds, Maggio thought he was about to lose his habitual self-control, but it didn't happen. An overly aggressive attitude hides fragility, he thought. Her lack of inhibition was devious, and love never is. When it came down to it, the lady had given herself away. But, of course, his ego had been invigorated.

«I'm delighted they think so,» he said, sliding to one side and heading towards the door. When he turned round, the lady was once more wearing her ordinary expression.

He said goodbye, allowing himself one last look at those beautiful legs. Sometimes clichés are not entirely banal, he thought.

Mrs Marecchia's husband was a farmer who lived along Via Orsoleto. For the first fifty years of his life he'd known nothing but sweat and toil on his farm. He had no brothers or sisters, no friends, he was jealous and a man of few words. Then he met this beautiful seductive girl, penniless, desirous of a roof over her head, and he'd decided to marry her so that he, too, could have one or more heirs. One evening, he unexpectedly returned home a couple of hours earlier than usual, and found the lady in their marriage bed with a young boy from who knows where. Youthful instinct made the boy the first to know what to do: he jumped out of the bed, grabbed his trousers with one hand and his shoes with the other, and dived through the ground floor window into the yard outside, then ran like crazy towards the road and from there to salvation in the melee at the beach. But Mr Marecchia wasn't particularly interested in him and headed towards his wife, lying paralyzed in the bed, not knowing what act to put on. She had no time to think of anything, on that occasion: two heavy whacks knocked her to the carpet. On getting to her feet, she felt her husband's horny right hand grab her neck, then push her into the small armchair next to the bed. There, Mr Marecchia stopped. A man of few words, and a few significant acts, he invited her to get dressed and leave for good, before dinner. Mrs Marecchia obediently got dressed and went to the carabinieri in Viserba.

«My husband beat me,» she said to the guard.

«Go to the emergency room and come back later,» was the response. «The maresciallo's not here at the moment.»

Mrs Marecchia went to the emergency room and as she waited her turn among the brawlers and the comatose drug addicts, she figured out how she could change the course of events, as always only apparently inescapable. She was medicated with a bandaid and a bit of disinfectant, a seven-day prognosis and plenty of paracetamol.

She left, went to the Carabinieri Headquarters in Rimini and said to the guard:

«My husband tried to kill me.»

The patrol car picked up Mr Marecchia while he was having dinner and late that night Mrs Marecchia fell asleep on the adulterous bed she was not supposed to see again. But the judge believed her husband, and a few days later granted him house arrest, enabling him to continue the same life, backwards and forwards between the fields and the house, as before the sad episode. The lady opposed it: it was the marital home, it was hers by right, dammit! But she became the victim of her own machinations: her husband had to stay in the house, she did not. So, for the second time in a few days, she left the bedroom as if for the last time, and took refuge in the boy's mini-apartment by the sea.

After a year of assiduous labour, to which he was accustomed, and increasingly infrequent checks, Mr Marecchia applied to get back his hunting license and the weapons confiscated the evening of the ugly deed. A hunter for more than thirty years, with never a sanction or a fine, he had no problems.

So that day, when for the first time after a dismal year he'd gone hunting again, he felt no great regret at seeing the pheasant escape; he knew he needed to recover a bit of rusted skill after the enforced pause. It was understandable that he didn't remember the positions and his favourite locations, just as it was possible that other hunters, no longer seeing him around, had turned up in precisely those places in which he used to lie in wait. Certainly, the strange package with the grey powder in it was a new thing for him. With a mixture of respect and the diffidence of the peasant farmer he didn't open it, because after all it wasn't his and if it was there, somebody must have put it there. Exactly: who, and why? He decided to put it in his bag and take it home, he'd think about it later.

On the other side of the river, two young men were searching for something, disoriented. They were both very nervous. Their emaciated faces, their sunken, dark-rimmed eyes, their pallor, the unnatural thinness of their young but already worn bodies, the scars - more or less hidden but all neglected, the swollen hands: everything proclaimed the fact that their only concern was to get hold of the daily dose of heroin required to ward off increasingly frequent episodes of withdrawal.

«I told you, we're on the wrong side,» said the first one.

«I don't remember ... maybe over there.»

They kept walking along the river bank for nearly a kilometre, until they reached the crossing. There they stopped.

«Let's go back along the other side. It all seemed very clear yesterday, but now I'm getting confused... «

The young man didn't remember that the day before he'd just had a hit and those few minutes of lucidity had been followed by a long period of fog which took him straight back to withdrawal. At that point, anything else became not secondary but superfluous, and only the search for a new dose justified every effort.

The shot rang out in the silence of the countryside. It came from close by; the pair looked at each other then, reanimated, headed for the place suggested to them by their ears. It took them at least ten minutes, their pace slowed by their inappropriate footwear and, more important, the weakness of limbs whose strength had been diminishing day by day for years. Only necessity drove them forward. When they got there, the younger of the two recognized the tree, and beneath it, the crude hide. They ran over to it without a word, then froze when they saw the loose soil, the empty hole, their precious consignment gone. The terror of the consequences of that disappearance chilled them to the bone; for long seconds neither of them said a word. It took, in rapid succession, a slammed door, a defective starter motor and the irregular sputter of a muffler in the distance to snap them out of it. They were just in time to see the little green jeep leave the dirt road and head towards the town.

Maggio took the phone from the guard and dialed Mrs Gaetana's number. Mrs Gaetana called every morning, because every night the neighbour's dog barked relentlessly and, according to her, somebody came too close to the fence. But there were never any burglaries or signs of an attempted break-in; at most, some female dog on heat wandering around. The problem would probably be over in a few days, Maggio told her, she needn't worry. With difficulty Mrs Gaetana made do with that simple prediction.

He was still explaining when the station bell rang. The guard went to open the door. Maggio, who had his back to it, turned round out of politeness. Somewhat startled, he thought how curious coincidences or chance could be, or perhaps someone took pleasure in weaving together the destinies of human beings. Mr Marecchia had just entered, a few minutes after his faithless ex-wife, when neither had ever, in all their lives, set foot inside the station before.

«I was hunting out of my shack,» he continued, «and I found this, by accident. I was going to give it to the chickens!»

«That'd be some roast dinner!» said Ponza.

Amazement immediately gave way to necessity.

«We must put it back,» said Maggio, «straight away. They'll soon come looking for it. We must hide it and wait. It won't take long.»

«Well, to tell the truth... I found it early this morning. I didn't think it was all that important...»

Maggio's heart sank at this last statement. A consignment like that wouldn't sit still for long. Hours, at most a day; too much fear of losing it, too great a need to sell it. Whoever had hidden it had to be very close by, even though it was probably already too late.

«Give me the package and wait here,» he said to Marecchia. «We'll go together.»

Maggio went to the office and put it in the safe, then went upstairs to the sleeping quarters. He looked into Ferro's room: he'd been on night shift and was still sleeping. Without a word, Maggio opened the window and threw back the shutters. The fresh air of the November morning did the rest. He went to his own room, took off his uniform and put on jeans and a T-shirt, then went into the kitchen and rummaged around in the pantry. The packet of whole wheat flour was still there, new and nearly past its expiry date. *Why do they bother buying it*, he thought. He found a plastic bag and went back. As he passed Ferro's room, he saw him moving around with considerable difficulty.

«Come on,» he said to him, «we've got to go and see a little something. Wear something practical!»

Ferro didn't complain, he never did, and began to get dressed.

Maggio went down the stairs, out of the building, and walked to the hairdresser's. Fortunately, there was no one else there when he arrived.

«Do you have a crimping iron you don't use anymore?»

A few minutes later, he left with the plastic bag. The welding job was a lot rougher than that of the unknown owners, but the dimensions were the same and the dark, the guilty haste of someone up to no good plus a bit of luck might just make it appear to be the original. Inside the package was a small tracking device that emitted a low-frequency radio signal; Ferro had put it together. It would work for at least two days, then the battery would run down.

Ferro and Marecchia were waiting for him in the street, each in their own car. Maggio nodded at Marecchia, who set off first. Their small and unlikely motorcade proceeded a fair way along the seafront road before heading inland. Several times, Maggio and Ferro exchanged a weary glance because of the speed of the small green jeep, low and constant, but once they were on the narrow country road, Ferro had to concentrate to keep their car on his trail, and after they turned into the grassy lane through the fields that led to the shack, it was a struggle not to lose sight of Marecchia, whose small car seemed to make its way from memory, avoiding every pothole and zigzagging across the track, even going up and down its sloping sides, without once braking or slackening its speed. Finally, the road ended in a grassy clearing half-hidden by trees and shrubs, a few meters from the river bank. The jeep had already stopped, its engine off; Marecchia had got out and was waiting for them.

«Over here,» he said, «it's not far.»

They walked along a narrow path until they came to where the wood ended. There, beneath a large oak tree, was a roof slung between two poles; a simple shelter, but functional and well knocked together. Marecchia stopped outside. «It's in there,» he said, pointing to the base of the nearest post, «a little hole the size of a shoe box.» Maggio went first; Ferro followed, the package of flour under his arm.

Amazement prevented any comments, what they saw didn't require it. Just inside the improvised shack, at their feet, was a hole, a metre square and at least 60 centimetres deep, that reached down to the robust roots of the oak tree above them. Dumbfounded, they stood there in silence, hands on their hips, suddenly feeling not observers but observed; not hunters any longer, but prey.

Cervi Park, a beautiful expanse of welcoming green in the centre of the city, was frequented, by day, by mothers and children and moderately intimate couples. By night, it became the destination of no-hopers and patrons of the most disparate types of drug. The two young guys were sitting on the backrest of a stone bench. Geo, the older of the two, was thinking, agitatedly, wondering what to do. The dose he'd just injected granted him a certain leeway, he was managing to articulate improbable plans of action. Max, twenty-two, was in the throes of a crisis, a combination of withdrawal and terror at the thought of the consequences of losing the consignment. *We just have to hang onto it until tonight*, Geo had told him, *it's a really easy job*; *there's a 1000 euros in it for us. You keep it, you don't have a record, then we take it back and that's it.* Geo was a longtime junkie: thefts, bagsnatching, robberies, and a lot of drugs, of all kinds. Too many for his thirty years. A lost life. Max had been using for three years; he'd started for no particular reason: because the opportunity presented or out of friendship, or bravado, he couldn't even remember. For him, the job wasn't all that easy. So, without saying a word, he'd taken the package to the shack and buried it there, and when they'd gone back to get it, it had vanished. They'd dug and dug: it was gone. But the Tunisian was already around and about and he wanted his stuff back; the unknown owner had to cut it and deliver it. His companions tended to use knives before they asked for explanations. For Max and Geo the situation was getting worse by the hour.

On their way back from the hunting shack, the three men stopped off for a coffee at the sports fishing lake. Here they said their goodbyes, each one returning to his own tasks. Mr Marecchia climbed back into his jeep and headed for home. He arrived, parked in the yard and walked towards the house.

Maggio and Ferro pondered what to do. They had placed the package of flour in the hole, taking care to make it look half-hidden by all the loosened soil. Even though they realized that whoever was supposed to come had already been there, they decided to go ahead with their plan. There wasn't much else they could do.

While Max watched the road, Geo slipped the screwdriver into the steering lock of the Vespa. One sharp blow and it disintegrated. He leapt on and started the engine. Without a word, Max got on behind him and they set off. Emboldened by the dose, they'd decided to go back. That shack belonged to somebody, some hunter. He'd be back, he'd keep on hunting. They would talk to him, they'd convince him, force him, threaten him; they'd do something. It was their stuff, for chrissake; and their ass. They found the road straight away, this time they were sufficiently lucid. The shack was still there, but the hole seemed smaller. Or bigger? The earth had been disturbed, at any rate, it looked different. What did that mean? And what was that half-concealed package? They looked at each other, puzzled. The package that had disappeared was now back. They knew that earlier on they'd been seriously out of it; maybe they hadn't searched thoroughly enough because of their anxiety, or their haste or whatever. They took the package and vanished in an instant; they would think about it all later.

Maggio and Ferro moved everything off the desk, then spread a plastic sheet over it. Ferro opened the wooden carrying case and carefully placed the little weighing scales in the centre of the sheet. They would need to take several measurements. Maggio took out a couple of vials of Narcotest, checking their expiry dates. They opened the package with a boxcutter then began to weigh its contents, using a cooking spoon. *Let's not forget to wash it before we put it back in the canteen*, they thought. One measuring cup contained 51 grams; they filled seven of them. The colour of the first test vial into which they'd dipped a tiny quantity of the substance turned yellow ochre, confirming what had seemed obvious from the start. They were looking at 357 grams of pure heroin, possibly part of a much bigger batch; the precise weight and the packaging testified to that. It wasn't a supermarket bag; it was high quality packaging plastic, sealed professionally, not with a hairdresser's iron. Duly cut, it would weigh at least four times as much; calculating four doses per gram times forty-fifty euros ...

«Well,» said Maggio, «someone's getting worried...»

In the caravan at the gypsy camp in the industrial area, the Tunisian seemed nowhere near convinced by the explanation Geo had just given him. Yes, he'd known him a long time; Geo had handled consignments for him on other occasions. He knew you could never trust an addict, in fact, you could never trust anybody, and he certainly didn't buy the story about the drug that disappeared then reappeared. Too many times he'd seen addicts succumb to the temptation to get rich quick, or be blackmailed into turning informer, in a scene where loyalty exists only to the habit or under threat of death. Before his eyes was a package, with a nicked corner, of whole wheat flour, or potato starch or whatever. He couldn't allow a small-time thug to steal his merchandise and go unpunished, and he certainly couldn't lose a consignment without saying or trying something. So he beckoned to one of the two guys standing behind him who had witnessed the silent meeting.

«Get the other guy, then go and have a look at the place they'll show you,» he said. Geo went outside, his eyes lowered and frightened, followed by the pair. He understood perfectly well that he was on the brink of the abyss. The chief nodded at the second guy, adding, in a lower voice, «Then you take care of them.» From the other end of the yard, Max watched the three of them emerge, undecided what to do. One of the thugs got into the car with Geo, the other headed towards his friend. With a single phrase, Geo the derelict redeemed a life of villainy.

«GO!» he yelled, waving his arms. «RUN FOR IT!»

Max's limbs stiffened, his eyes widened. He had a moment's hesitation, but a huge rush of adrenaline did away with his conscience; more lucid than he'd been for years, he turned, started the Vespa and shot out of the yard onto the road like a rocket, then hurtled uncatchable onto the nearby highway and immediate salvation. They'd seen him, of course, but they didn't know who he was, he only needed to keep out of sight for a while and no one would find him.

From the door of the trailer, the Tunisian grimaced in disapproval, then looked at the car. One of the thugs held Geo by the collar, the other had grabbed hold of a large knife. Both were waiting for instructions.

«*Allez*,» he ordered, and went back inside. He glanced again at the package of flour on the table, then sat himself down on the sofa and turned on the satellite TV.

For the third time in a few hours, Geo found himself near the shack. They'd had to leave the old Mercedes some way off because the dirt road was too rough. So when they heard the sound of the small jeep manoeuvring in the distance, it took a while for them to race back to the car. They didn't need to ask Geo: anyone who took that road was heading for the shack. If that person was also driving the green jeep Geo had told them about, panting and gesticulating wildly, well, few doubts remained. All three had clearly seen the license plate, and he couldn't go far in that old vehicle. They got into the car and reversed back along the road at full throttle, ignoring potholes, puddles and suspension. Following the trail of fresh soil that had dropped off the 4WD's wheels they ended up heading in the right direction. Finally, as they were roving around the adjacent country roads, they saw the jeep in the large courtyard of an old farmhouse. They parked out of sight. One of them got out, and walked past the gate; beneath the street number, 9/b, was a mailbox with a name on it: Marecchia. He got out his phone and called the boss.

Ferro raced up the stairs. «Maggio!» he called out, knocking on the bathroom door. «Maggio! Come downstairs, the location of the tracking device has changed.» Maggio, swearing under his breath, finished what he was doing and went down to the floor below. The rudimentary transmitter Ferro had assembled was doing its duty, the beep alerting them that the signal had changed, the red light now brighter telling them that the package was a little closer, in the same area. They rushed out, having decided to go back to the land around the shed and start from there.

The boss ended the call, put the phone down and pressed *mute* again on the remote control. Al Jazeera resumed emitting 60 words a minute, but the Tunisian stood up and turned it off at the switch. He picked up an apple and reflected. A house like that had a thousand hiding places, they could search it for days and find nothing. The guy wasn't a criminal, maybe they could try a different approach. He consulted the phone book and found: Marecchia, Via ... 9/b. He dialed the number. A male voice answered, adult, a Romagnolo accent. It could be him.

«Hello? Hello?! Is anyone there? Hello?» The voice betrayed anxiety; if he'd thought it was a wrong number, he would have already hung up, thought the boss. He waited a few more seconds, then he spoke.

«You want trouble? Money?»

The party on the other end had been struck dumb. The silence lasted a few long seconds, then the boss ended the call and took a bite of the apple.

Marecchia was left holding the receiver, perplexed. It wasn't that he was afraid, his farming life was inspired by completely different rules; an ancient equilibrium reassured and supported him. He didn't even know what the fellow was talking about, and anyway he didn't want either one or the other. His conscience dictated that he notify the police, however, just as he'd gone to them the day before. He turned off the gas leaving the saucepan with the pancetta and the beans, plenty of them, oily and soaked in sauce the way he liked them, on the gas ring, put on his jacket and went out. The three in the Mercedes, parked just far enough away, saw him leave in his little green car and notified the boss.

«We'd better turn back,» said Ferro, his eyes fixed on the small screen.

«Why?» asked Maggio.

«If we go this way the signal fades out.»

«But the shack is straight ahead!»

«Turn round, come on. We'll try further on.»

Maggio pulled over and prepared to do a U-turn, but it wasn't easy on the highway, so they had to keep going until they got to the roundabout, a kilometre further on, then turn back. By then, the signal had become so weak it had faded almost to nothing.

They gazed at the little LED with some apprehension. But after they'd done the U-turn and returned to their starting point, the signal resumed, and it kept getting stronger as they headed south. At the crossroads with Via Emilia, they had to make a choice.

«Do we go straight ahead or do we turn?»

«Let's turn into Via Emilia,» said Maggio, «it's green on the right.»

«What if it's straight on?»

«We'll drive around the industrial zone for a bit, then get back onto the highway further on.»

Mrs Marecchia had been restless for several days. She'd got out of bed leaving her young lover deep in a well-deserved sleep and was wandering around the small studio apartment. At the time, it had seemed like a palace, but now it seemed more and more cramped with each passing day. Truth to tell, the house business had stuck in her craw. She had to live with this boy while her husband had her house all to himself. Her house, of course. She had to resolve the question and she knew, and knew well, only one way of doing that. Silently, she dressed and went out, straight to the farmhouse. She was determined to confront him. She would tell him she was angry, that he'd neglected her, that the boy had been so insistent, taking advantage of her momentary weakness and the naivety of a woman willing to believe that love can be found anywhere. She knew he would listen to her in silence, as always; he would understand and, ultimately, forgive her and take her back into her home. At that point, she'd be able to regain control of the situation and think about the future; an immediate future in which she would have to sever all ties, of course, but later, with time and a little adroitness, she'd be able to revive and resume the relation, less assiduously, certainly, too big a commitment for a woman in her position, destined as soon as possible to manage the farm. She smiled as she anticipated that soon, very soon, she'd be returning to her home.

The Mercedes parked badly just outside the gate forced her to deal with reality once more. It wouldn't let her past, much less inside. She began to honk the horn and yell.

«Is anybody there? Would you move this car?!»

Inside the house, where they'd turned everything upside down, Geo and the two Tunisians froze. Without a word, they climbed out of the window through which they'd entered. Apparently anyone who frequented the house, for whatever reason, recognized the window as the escape route. Mrs Marecchia saw them come racing towards her and, congratulating herself on the fact that they'd been so quick to take up her invitation, she stuck her head out the window and yelled maliciously:

«*Bravi*! About time! What were you thinking?»

All three ignored her, got into the car, and tore off at great speed.

As soon as he'd ended the call, the boss got up and went to the door. He'd given clear instructions to his men; while waiting for something to happen, it's best not be found, on principle. He mounted the bike and headed out of the gypsy camp. Who was going to stop a poor ragged Tunisian on a bicycle with a bag of apples in his front basket at six in the evening? He passed amid the indifference of the Roma kids absorbed in smoking and the adults watching them. At that very moment, Maggio and Ferro were driving along the parallel street.

«The signal's incredibly strong,» said Ferro.

«Let's drop in on the gypsy camp,» said Maggio.

«The indicator's already as high as it goes.»

Ferro honked at the North African wobbling on his bicycle to get out of the way, then entered the parking lot and stopped in the middle of the yard, among the caravans.

The smell was perceptible; fires were always burning inside tin drums, heating the air whatever the season, incinerating everything thrown into them.

No one moved, nobody stopped what they were doing; as far as they were concerned, Maggio, Ferro and the official car had the same consistency as the air around them. Watching a tree grow would have aroused more alarm in those present.

Maggio and Ferro got out, looked around, then started wandering through the temporary shanties and the shacks on wheels. The two marescialli knew that drugs were not a gypsy thing, but the tracking device was displaying a deep fixed red. They ruled out the family dwellings, the kids with the gold rings, the toothless old women, and after casting a quick glance inside and underneath the caravans, they arrived together at the only one that was locked, at the end. It had no license plate, and no VIN number on the tow bar. On closer inspection, it wasn't shabby either, unlike the others. On top, was a satellite antenna; in front, on the ground, an oriental-style carpet; nearby, a pair of sandals. It looked like a makeshift place of worship. Without a word, they pressed their faces against two different windows, shading their eyes with their hands to block out the reflections. Inside, was a single bed and a plasma TV on pause; in the middle, a small table with a remote control sitting next to a half-open bag of flour.

Geo had grasped the situation very well. He had few doubts about the likely outcome, and when one of the thugs moved from the front seat to the back and sat down beside him, even those evaporated. No drugs, no chance of walking away alive; they weren't going to let him get away with it, weren't going to swallow some junkie's tall tales about the disappearance of a major consignment. True or not, they had to make an example of him; everyone in the drug scene would be given confirmation that the Tunisian didn't mess around, if proof were needed. So, as soon as the car slowed down, without having worked out any sort of plan but simply gripped by an irrepressible instinct to escape, identical to that of the rats who abandon a sinking ship or a burning burrow, he opened the door and threw himself out. He rolled on the gravel then into the ditch, while the cars on the highway, full of sunburnt bathers and gleeful kids, sped by, indifferent. Inwardly, he smiled at the ease with which he'd managed that athletic manoeuvre, with very little damage, all things considered, as he watched the Mercedes pull away at full speed, oblivious to him. No damage; only, thinking back, a twinge as he opened the door, like a cold burn, swift and sharp in his left side. He looked down and his face went pale; a red spot was spreading over his white t-shirt. He lifted it up: blood was flowing copiously from between two flaps of skin. Suddenly, in his mind's eye, he saw the rusty knife again, in the hand of that worst of traveling companions, then felt the twinge again and the pain. But now, as if by magic, the preoccupations of an ill-spent life were fading; a sense of well-being pervaded his worn limbs and a repose he had forgotten returned to console him. On his knees, he saw his mother take him in her arms. Finally safe, he abandoned himself to that supreme love, slumped to the ground and, with a faint smile, closed his eyes forever.

From behind a bush not far away, Max had seen the Mercedes drive off and the body fall, rise unsteadily to its feet for a few moments then fall again and move no more. He saw one or two cars slow down and cast a quick look at the drunken bum asleep on the side of the road. Finally, he saw a car stop, the occupants get out and, waving their arms, raise the alarm. He then got up from his temporary shelter and, desperate but lucid, tried to organize a rapid plan of reaction to everything that had happened in the last few hours. He could feel the withdrawal coming on, too; the effect of the drug was ebbing and he would soon need another hit. Contradictory sentiments, a mixture of fear, gratitude and remorse, prevented him from thinking clearly. He took out his phone and dialed a number.

Maggio turned round to suggest something to Ferro, and was just in time to see him ram the door of the trailer with his shoulder and go inside. It certainly wasn't the flimsy lock that made that improvised dwelling secure, but rather the unwritten pact of non-aggression between the Tunisians and the gypsies. Maggio gave a snort of disapproval. *He could have waited*, he thought. Just then, his cell phone rang. It was Ponza, the guard.

«Maresciallo!»

«Yes, what is it?»

«Maresciallo, they found a corpse with stab wounds near the highway, on the road to the shack, I think.»

«Damn, that's just near here!»

«Yes, maresciallo, and then...»

He was interrupted by the squeal of tyres. The Mercedes was returning to base, at breakneck speed; obviously the two thugs were in a hurry to inform the boss and get out of there. They didn't know he had already made his own arrangements. At the sight of Maggio's official car and, above all, the wide-open door of the caravan, the driver stopped in the middle of the yard, undecided what to do. As if in a grotesque piece of popular theatre, the good guys and the bad guys were facing off before an unusual audience, the indifferent but totally attentive gypsies.

The first to speak was Maggio:

«Were you the ones who called?»

That was the best line he could think of, and this time it was Ferro who gazed at him disconsolately.

The pair didn't fall for it; they'd been intending to look for their boss, but under those circumstances instinct prevailed. The world is full of bosses to serve. The reverse light came on and the Tunisian rammed his foot down on the accelerator.

Ferro plunged in, drew his gun and pointed it at the pair while Maggio ran to get the official car.

«Stop!» he ordered.

They didn't stop; on the contrary, they accelerated in the direction of the exit, swerving so hard in an effort to head for the gate that they ended up crashing into a string of tin drums. The car remained stuck for a few seconds and when the inept driver managed to set off again, foot to the boards, he found Maggio's car in front of him, sideways on. Maggio just managed to leap into the passenger seat before the Mercedes smashed into the poor old Fiat Punto, putting an end to that short and desperate attempt at a getaway.

The two Tunisians got out, dazed by the impact. Maggio and Ferro were on top of them immediately and immobilized them. A body search produced two very sharp knives, one soiled with blood. On the back seat of the Mercedes they found fresh blood stains.

Finally, two more patrol cars arrived. The arrested men were taken to the station, there were still a few things to clear up. Ferro retrieved his artisanal tracking device; the bare interior of the caravan hid nothing else. He went outside and waited for the tow truck to haul away the two damaged cars.

As Maggio was leaving, he saw the kids going into the North Africans' trailer as they pleased. The pact was no longer in force.

Just then, Ponza called.

«Yes, go ahead.»

«As I was saying, shortly after that a guy called; he didn't say who he was. He said he saw the two Tunisians in the Mercedes throw Geo out of the car; that's what he called him, Geo ... «

Maggio interrupted him.

«Yes, we're here! Notify headquarters, tell them we're on our way back.»

First, though, they passed by the place where the corpse was. The specialist personnel were already scouring the area; Maggio had no reason to remain. But he recognized Geo at first sight.

As soon as he got back to the station, Maggio checked the log of incoming calls on the office landline. There was one cell phone number; he logged in to the provider's customer register: it belonged to Max. A local junkie, no different from many others. They would never know every detail but the pieces were all on the table: the drugs, the dealers, the scores to settle, the unexpected event. Of course, the testimony of this unknown person who had called them might clarify a lot of the details.

Maggio immediately sent out a patrol car to look for Max, while he took care of the two Tunisians.

A small crowd of passers-by and onlookers had gathered to follow the operations of the tow truck. Some were even sitting on the edge of the footpath nearby, making themselves comfortable. In the background, the imperturbable gypsies were preparing dinner. Among the impromptu audience, the boss was also watching, unsmiling. There was no way they could trace anything back to him. His two henchmen knew him only as the «boss.» He climbed on his bike and headed away towards the city. Halfway there, he stopped on a little bridge over a culvert, took out his phone, and removed the battery and the SIM card. The device finished up in the muddy water. He then resumed his pedaling and, in the middle of the road, let the card slip down onto the asphalt: the passing cars would ensure it was destroyed. Finally, he stopped next to a recycling bin and threw in the battery. A little further on, he leaned his bike against a fence and collected his thoughts. His cover was blown by now, but his network was intact. He would continue his lucrative trade in death without further inconveniences. He took an apple from the basket and began to eat it with quiet satisfaction.

It was almost dinner time when the patrol car arrived at Max's place. It was a modest country home, everything on the ground floor. Max's father, a farmer, came out to greet them, composed resignation on his face.

«You're here already,» he said.

The two carabinieri looked at each other, nonplussed.

He gestured to them to follow him out the back. They walked along a narrow footpath; as soon as they rounded the corner, the man stopped and stood back, looking straight ahead of him.

«That's how I found him,» he said, his outstretched palm accompanying his words. «...a thing like that...» he added. Then he stopped, unable to find other words. There was no need. The carabinieri hesitated; they were used to it, but you never get used to it. They were pervaded by a sense of sympathy and compassion for that man so impotent in the face of misfortune.

Max was there, just a couple of metres away, hanging by the neck, strangled by the leather belt of his own trousers, firmly anchored to the top of the window frame in his own bedroom, his knees bent slightly forward, his toes just touching the floor, no longer able to bear weight of any kind.

Maggio was notified shortly after. With the two arrested men in jail, there was nothing more to add to that mournful day. By now it was dark; he lit a cigarette and leaned on the sill of the window that overlooked the sea. Among other things, Maggio had a little niggling doubt, there was something that didn't quite fit: when he looked inside the caravan, before the rambunctious arrival of the Mercedes, he'd seen only one chair in front of the plasma TV; on the coffee table, one paper cup and a few apples; nearby, one plate with a core on it; behind it, one single unmade bed; outside, one mat and one pair of sandals. Only one person lived there, he concluded. Which of the two wasn't clear, since they seemed to move and act in unison. The thing left him not entirely at ease, but it was a doubt that would be difficult to resolve. The two Tunisians didn't seem very inclined to talk. He would request the details of their phone traffic and Marecchia's, certainly; but it would take time. And then, too, Maggio was wary of the so-called empirical evidence, the evidence that demonstrates only its own existence; he considered a look and a motive to be the same order of evidence as the blood, the knife and the drug, though the former were difficult to prove.

His thoughts were interrupted by Ferro, just back, who called to him from the tow truck. «Want to go for a pizzetta? Nacio's coming too!»

Nacio was the owner of the authorised panelbeating firm. Like all good Riminese, he never refused an invitation.

Maggio stood there for a moment, then decided that enough was enough.

«Coming,» he replied, and joined them in the truck.

Mr Marecchia was astonished to see the car of his by now ex-wife parked outside his house. Going inside, he found her sitting on the couch, her skirt hitched slyly above mid-thigh. Thus distracted, he barely noticed the mess.

«I thought you might be feeling lonely,» began the lady, with no trepidation whatsoever.

Mr Marecchia was unfazed. He took off his jacket and hung it up, then returned to the kitchen to pick up where he'd left off, and relit the gas burner.

Behind him, the lady's silhouette partially blocked the light through the doorway. Out of the corner of his eye, he saw her slip off her dress. From behind, she put one arm around his waist, while with the other hand she stroked his head.

Mr Marecchia had a moment of hesitation, then he turned round and returned her embrace. They swapped positions in increasingly lewd contortions until the lady, her head resting on his shoulder, betrayed her malign intentions with an unequivocal smile, then closed her eyes, thinking it had been easier than expected. That was precisely the moment when she felt something warm on her head, something more and more fragrant and intense; it smelt like... pancetta?!?! She recoiled in disgust as her ex-husband's dinner, full of garlic, oil, fried peperoncino and rosemary, dripped from her hair down her suntanned and beautiful naked back. She screeched with vexation as she fled ignominiously, snatching up her dress from the ground amid the sonorous laughter of Mr Marecchia, who followed her every step of the way, watching her clumsy attempts to get dressed with her eyes closed and irritated, whether by the practical joke or the sauce was hard to tell. And so she went out forever, with her soiled clothes and soul, from the house and the life of Mr Marecchia.

Maggio, Ferro and Nacio had just finished the first portion of *spiedini*. To tell the truth, Ferro's appetite was unbeatable, and Nacio was no slouch either. Maggio was not a big eater, but he usually managed to hold his own. That evening, however, he had very little appetite. Tragic events always left him wondering. Could they have avoided it? He still didn't know.

Mazza served the *fornarine* still steaming, and everybody's attention returned to the good things in life: food, the heart, the bed; above all, what would happen in the next five minutes, because tomorrow, in all its unpredictability, would be something else again.

Just then, Ferro waggled his head at him.

«Someone's looking for you,» he said.

Maggio turned around, and saw her Mini stopped in the courtyard.

But he decided that he needed a little more time; yes, all the time it would take to see the bottom of his plate.

Notes

Did you like this story?

Did you come across any typos?

Is there anything you'd like to ask me?

You can leave a review on my *Smashwords page*

or comment on my blog and visit or *Like* my Facebook page

***

Italian and Spanish version available!

***

Maresciallo Maggio also stars in the thrillers

«Dangerous Game, Maresciallo Maggio»

«Dirty Business, Maresciallo Maggio!»

in the collection of prequel short stories:

«There's Always a Reason, Maresciallo Maggio!» (Italian and French edition available)

in the serialized novel *«Choices»*

and the short story *«Regrets»*

***

(The third story in the collection, *«Addressee Unknown»* was first published in No. 3061 of the Giallo Mondadori magazine, ,and appears courtesy of the magazine *«Il carabiniere»*)

***

Maresciallo Maggio will be back in the novel:

«The Hero»

***

Do you like contemporary history?

I am the author of the historical novel *«The Choice»,* set in Rome between October 6-16, 1943, when the Jewish Ghetto was raided and its residents deported to the camps...

***

Looking for an original gift? Give a signed copy of my book: read how on my blog!

***

English versions soon available for every book!

Sommario

Characters 2

INTRODUCTION 5

THE TELLTALE PHONE 7

A NASTY BUSINESS 21

ADDRESSEE UNKNOWN 36

Notes 63

CPSIA information can be obtained at www.ICGtesting.com
Printed in the USA
LVOW04s2115300815

452108LV00022B/872/P